TO SEE OUT THE NIGHT

David Clerson

TO SEE OUT
THE NIGHT

Translated from the French by Katia Grubisic

QC FICTION

Revision: Peter McCambridge
Proofreading: David Warriner, Elizabeth West
Book design: Folio infographie
Cover & logo: Maison 1608 by Solisco
Fiction editor: Peter McCambridge

ISBN 978-1-77186-268-4 pbk; 978-1-77186-269-1 epub;
978-1-77186-270-7 pdf
Legal Deposit, 3rd quarter 2021
Bibliothèque et Archives nationales du Québec
Library and Archives Canada

Published by QC Fiction, an imprint of Baraka Books
Printed and bound in Québec

TRADE DISTRIBUTION & RETURNS
Canada - UTP Distribution: UTPdistribution.com
United States & World - Independent Publishers Group: IPGbook.com

We acknowledge the financial support for translation and promotion of the Société de développement des entreprises culturelles (SODEC), the Government of Québec tax credit for book publishing administered by SODEC, the Government of Canada, and the Canada Council for the Arts.

Société de développement des entreprises culturelles
Québec

Financé par le gouvernement du Canada
Funded by the Government of Canada | Canadä

"I will desert your armies. I will freely circulate in the intermediate space."

– Claude Cahun, translated by S. de Muth

TABLE OF CONTENTS

THE APE WITHIN

ON JANUARY 6, 2016, Louis, a night watchman, lost his job in a downtown parking lot after he let in a homeless man. The man was hunched over, and a messy beard covered half his face. He smelled revolting. Louis felt sorry for him, and didn't say anything when the man walked by his booth, watching as he shuffled into the depths of the parking garage. Three floors down he fell asleep over a heating grate. When he woke up he shat, leaning against a Mercedes and smearing the car with his excrement.

Louis didn't really try very hard to find other work. He had a little money saved up, and his employment insurance benefits were good enough. At first he hung out with a few former colleagues with whom he used to go for a beer, but he stopped answering their emails, and they stopped asking him along. Although it was cold, he spent his days walking across the city, through Jarry Park, along the train tracks, and up to the top of the mountain, sometimes staying until nightfall.

At night, on Chambord Street not far from the Metropolitan expressway, he ate pasta, sitting alone at his kitchen table, his computer open in front of him. He usually watched nature documentaries, on bears or hyenas, lampreys, other animals. Maybe it was a way of revisiting his childhood, the fascination he'd had for exotic beasts, or trying to relive his university years. He had briefly taken biology because he thought he wanted to be a zoologist, though he gave up in the end. As his schoolwork became less important and he got used to the routine and the atmosphere of the underground parking garage, he let the night-watchman gig take over.

One evening in April, four months after he was fired, he was watching a documentary on endangered species of Southeast Asia when an orangutan appeared on the screen, a hulking male squatting heavily on a branch. The camera panned along the ape's body: the wide facial disc, its texture like leather, and the tiny eyes shoved deep into the skin, as if they were about to disappear. Louis met the animal's stare, those eyes in which he saw nothing, a blankness that frightened him. Although other images blinked across the screen, Louis felt that his gaze remained plunged into the orangutan's, that the dark eyes were a parasite inside him, as if the primate's pupils had lodged themselves in his.

Louis's body was racked with shivers. His chest grew tight, his fingers shook. He suddenly hated the reek of his breath, which smelled like an animal's. That night he had trouble falling asleep, and woke shortly before dawn convinced that the orangutan now lived within him.

In the days that followed, Louis felt his limbs growing languorous. They no longer seemed to move the same way; his gestures seemed at once more fluid and much slower. His habits changed. He almost never went out, only to get groceries on Jarry, and he started spending less time online. One Saturday at the beginning of May he dropped his fork on the floor and found himself eating with his hands. The next day he injured his shoulder after trying to hang from his shower-curtain rod, which ripped out of the wall from his weight. A few days after that, he woke up wet, which hadn't happened since childhood. He decided that the incontinence wasn't him; it was the ape within that had needed to urinate. His sheets and his mattress were wet too, and the next night he decided to sleep on the floor in a nest of blankets.

The other anthropoid showed itself gradually. It wasn't so much the sometimes out-of-control behaviour that worried Louis, but the feeling of a presence that was growing inside him, and taking up all the space. His limbs hurt. Sometimes he woke up in the night thinking his skin was tearing. Every day he ran his hands over his body, squeezing his arms and legs as if to make sure they belonged to him. Louis could feel the ape stretching within him, the ape's joints moving, the ape's head thinking inside his own. Its proportions were almost human; the ape filled his entire body. Sometimes it seemed like the orangutan would kill him, that it was feeding on him from the inside. At other times Louis had the impression that what was growing under his skin was the emptiness left by an animal dying. He saw again the dark face, the eyes. He was lost in the orangutan's small bright eyes, and he imagined being inhabited by a dying animal.

Several times Louis shoved his fingers down his throat, as if he could vomit out the ape, but he only spat up a trickle of saliva. He wondered what effect abortion pills would have, or whether he should try some kind of antiparasitic instead. He also thought of his father's gun—his father, who'd been a hunter—and he visualized pushing the gun all the way into his mouth to kill the ape. But that would accomplish nothing; to dislodge it he first had to get to know the foreign presence.

The summer was unbearably hot. Louis's apartment was an oven, and he sat in the sweltering heat reading about primates. He learned that orangutans were solitary and territorial, that they ate fruit, shoots, eggs, insects, and invertebrates, and that they were constantly on the move, building a new nest of branches every night. The cries of the males were powerful, and could carry over a kilometre or more. Louis could almost hear them in the distance. The fangs of an ape in one photograph terrified him. He saw others, victims of hunters or held in poacher cages. What struck him most was a piece he read on animal trafficking. The exotic-animals trade was strictly regulated, and in some countries offenders were punished with jail time, but across the world, the market brought in millions. Hidden in the trunks of cars, in the holds of ships, or in the back of delivery trucks, all kinds of creatures were being smuggled across borders—reptiles, rainbow-feathered birds, felines, amphibians, monkeys. Orangutan babies were especially sought after as pets. Separated from their mothers, most died during the journey. Some were rescued by border guards but they were too young and couldn't be released back into the wild.

Although Louis had never left the country, he knew the Canada–US border's reputation: American customs officials were tough. A former colleague of Louis's, Rawi, who was Lebanese, had been turned away when he tried to go on vacation in Maine. Louis figured that venomous spiders or reptiles could get across pretty easily, and maybe smaller primates, like lemurs or marmosets, but a big ape would be difficult to sneak over the border. He had to get to the United States as soon as possible.

That evening he found a rental agency online, with an office less than a kilometre from his place, and he reserved a car. He found his passport in a drawer under a pile of socks, without a single stamp. He didn't sleep that night, spending most of it in front of his computer. He read about exotic-animal trafficking laws, and felt better. The next day Louis drove to the States.

Sweat poured down his forehead. He gripped the steering wheel, but his limbs felt like they were being stretched from the inside out, and his fingers were too tight. Three times he stopped to pee, afraid that the ape would force him to urinate. The border crossing seemed to take forever. When the customs officers asked him why he was going, he said something vague about the beaches of Maine and New Hampshire, the Bronx Zoo, a zoo in Queens. He was surprised that they let him through, even as the ape stirred within him. He could feel his heart beating in his head. His skin was slick with sweat. But as soon as he set foot on American soil, a weight lifted from his shoulders. He laughed unexpectedly, suddenly convinced that the orangutan had been intercepted at the border.

Louis pulled over on the side of the road. He took a deep breath, folded and unfolded his hands and rubbed them over his face. He stuck out his tongue in his rearview mirror. He was free. He couldn't remember ever feeling so light.

He slept in a motel near the interstate. He drank beer in front of the TV and ate a hamburger and fries coated with ketchup and mayonnaise. Louis rarely drank. Although he had sometimes had one too many with guys from work, his drunkenness had always been circumstantial. That evening, however, he downed one beer after another. When he finished the cans he'd bought, he went to the motel bar and came back with a bottle of cheap whiskey. He was drinking, he was drunk; he was drunk and he was laughing, he was surprised by his own laughter. He lay back on the bed and flipped through American reality shows, the secret life of Britney Spears, a story about a refugee boat sinking in the Mediterranean.

When he woke up, the screen was still flashing. It took a long time to find the remote control to click the TV off. Louis's head was on fire, and he wanted to throw up. He had dark circles under his eyes. His face was pale, his limbs leaden, his mouth pasty. Everything about him disgusted him. He wanted to go back to sleep, but couldn't. It occurred to him that the orangutan's disappearance hadn't freed him. Now he was suffering from the animal's absence, he'd been abandoned.

At eleven o'clock a hotel clerk knocked on his door: time to check out. He decided to pay for another night, and asked for some ibuprofen. After taking a couple of pills, he was able to sleep. When he opened his eyes, it was night again.

In a dream he'd climbed mangroves and meranti trees, screaming under the branches and ripping into the flesh of exotic fruits. His arms were agile. On the mossy ground of a swampy forest, he had copulated with a female. He was awake now, and went into the bathroom to splash water on his face. In the mirror he stared at his black eyes, and he thought he recognized the eyes of the ape. He stretched out his hands and opened his mouth wide. When he raised his arms over his head, he was surprised to find them so long, and he laughed again. He knew that the orangutan was still living in him, clinging to his body. The animal had been able to get across after all. In hindsight, Louis was perplexed that he'd wanted the orangutan to leave at all. He'd felt so deserted when he thought the ape had left. He wanted to learn to live with the other.

The rest of the story is a rebirth. Back home, Louis bought ferns, alocasias, and hibiscus to decorate his apartment. His diet changed, and he ate nuts and fruit rather than the omelettes, rice, or pasta that had once been his staples. He felt stronger, more alert, more confident. Sometimes, usually shortly after waking up, it seemed to him that the orangutan was overflowing, pouring out over his body, that it engulfed him. He thought he was carrying out a mission, as if he'd found in the ape an answer to his life.

One evening in August, he was listening to an expert online who explained that orangutans would be extinct within ten years from poaching and habitat loss. *There is no hope*, the biologist said, but for Louis the words were a revelation: the species would survive in him.

His apartment looked like a jungle. He patted dirt everywhere, and plants started growing along the walls. Sometimes he defecated on the floor. He never washed or changed his clothes anymore, and his beard and hair were long and dirty. His appearance and his smell were repulsive. When he went out, people avoided him. He liked the disgust and the fear he elicited. To those around him, it looked like Louis was losing it.

At night he dreamed of Borneo, but by day he never thought of returning to the forest, where the last wild primates would perish. He rejoiced: exile was a refuge for the ape, and it gave meaning to his legs, arms, belly, and head.

The rest might seem obvious. Louis was evicted from his apartment, Louis ended up on the street, eating out of the garbage, Louis was cloaked in his filth. He sometimes thought he was dressed as a monkey. Louis caught scabies and Lyme disease, Louis lived out a few summers and winters before he was found dead in the middle of the detritus. What's less predictable is that before he died, he prowled across a strange, unnameable Earth. He lived among humans like a beast. His feet were prehensile and his arms even longer than orangutans' arms, his blackened skin became leathery, his head grew wider. As his understanding of reality changed, he thought he could glimpse the delirious landscapes of worlds to come, where he roamed, half-man, half-ape, beneath the sultry sun that set the earth and the sky ablaze.

I'd worked with him for a long time, and I saw him now and again during the last years of his life. He wandered downtown, and he often walked by the entrance to the underground parking lot where I still worked. I always said hello. Most of the time he avoided me, but sometimes he would whisper what was going through his head, bits and pieces of his life.

I saw him one last time shortly before his death. I was walking down an alley between Stanley and Peel on my way home from work as the sun came up when I saw something moving through the garbage. At first I stepped back. But I recognized him, and I went over. I can hardly repeat what he said to me, his words were so garbled, but my eyes met his. I saw a deep darkness, an emptiness into which I started to sink. I believe his eyes were acknowledging the imminence of death. Just as I was about to leave, to leave him to the squalor, I was afraid his eyes had inseminated me, just as the ape's eyes had inseminated him. He would die within me as he died amid the trash, and his death would settle inside of me.

YAMACHICHE

PAUL DERAPS first started writing after reading Kafka and Beckett, to whose work a cégep
instructor in Trois-Rivières had introduced him.
Deraps quit school shortly thereafter—he'd been
studying mechanical engineering—and moved
back to Yamachiche. He never left. He lived off
social assistance and did odd jobs, clearing snow
from the steps of an old folks' home or picking
up fieldstones. As a teenager he'd spent hours
with medieval fantasy sagas borrowed from the
library, but now, this time, he brought his new
favourite authors from Trois-Rivières, and read
them over and over.

Deraps never lacked imagination, but writing
wasn't easy for him. He picked his titles and the

topics of his books, but he struggled to actually write them. On a Compaq Deskpro inherited from his father, he started *The Time of the Dog*, *Where the Murmurs Die*, *Years of Darkness*, *Anthracite*, *Awakening of the Beasts*, *The Eye of the Bog*, *A Conspiracy of Snails*, and *The Imagination of Bipeds*—novels that he never finished. It should be noted that Paul drank a lot, often to the point of not being able to write at all. He ate too much too, and loved fatty foods, which he consumed in excess, even though digestion leads to sleep rather than to inspiration. Yet until the age of thirty he managed to continue his literary activities, drafting *What Do the Crayfish Dream?*, *The Spider Shrew*, *The Miracle of Strangulation*, *Slaughterhouse Mechanical*, *Hang the Octopus*, *The Ailing Sky*, *Divination of the Hanged*, and *Tongue Cancer*. He wrote as he got progressively drunker, and his texts became increasingly just a spewing of words—page after page of shapeless statements and twilight allegories in which men degenerated and merged with animals and the earth. Paul died at thirty, just as he'd begun writing *Rot in the Brain of the Rotten*. He was staggering along the 138 with a bottle of Jack Daniel's in his hand when he was hit by a Ford pickup truck going over one-twenty.

His sister didn't find out he was dead until after the funeral. For almost six years she'd been living in Lucerne, in the German-speaking part of Switzerland, squatting in an abandoned bourgeois house in a wooded area on the edge of town. The house was occupied by about fifteen young anarchists—Swiss, Italians, two Croats, a few French people, and one girl from Quebec. They held punk concerts in the cellar. A massive plaster vagina hung above the stage. Everyone drank heavily.

Before she left for Switzerland, Rebecca Deraps, influenced by her brother, had also given herself over to writing. Paul was two years older than she was, and he used to make her read his drafts before she left Yamachiche for Montreal. Rebecca had dropped out of high school three times. She didn't get along with her mother— their arguments were legendary—and Rebecca obviously had a problem with authority. She moved to the city at nineteen, and enrolled in art at the Cégep du Vieux-Montréal, but her main goal was getting student loans. Rebecca lived on Parthenais with five roommates, including Claire, a friend who was seriously ill. The two became lovers, and Rebecca nursed Claire to the end of her life. It was after Claire's death that Rebecca started writing. Her only book was entitled *Riot Inside*, a prose text written in a single block with no punctuation, paragraphs, or chapters, describing the tensions within a humongous creature whose diseased organs swell, contaminate, and infect each other. It was intended to be about systemic violence that ultimately stands as a metaphor for social struggle. The piece was more or less unreadable, but a nihilistic hatred of political and economic structures was ferociously evident, as was, more broadly, a disgust for civilization, for notions of nationhood, authority, and progress. Rebecca didn't send it out to publishers; she self-published it as a zine, printing thirty copies. Ten were handed out at a punk concert held in an apartment on Saint-Hubert, and most of those ended up trampled or soaked in beer. Of the two copies that night that avoided this fate, one happened to fall into the hands of a junkie, who tried to sell it on Sainte-Catherine and failed, dumping it in the snow. One of Rebecca's childhood friends kept the other; he was another kid from Yamachiche, and utterly lost in Montreal, where he'd come to visit her. He went home the next day with the memory of a chaotic night, the likes of which he would never see again. Of the rest, five copies ended up in the Cégep du Vieux-

Montréal student association office and were unfortunately tossed, along with a pile of anarcho-communist leaflets. Ten other copies, which Rebecca had given to the friend who'd illustrated the cover, burned in a house fire on Christophe-Colomb. A month after publishing the zine, the five remaining copies flew to Paris with Rebecca. She had just fallen in love with Hann Zimmer, a Swiss-German guitarist whose concert she'd caught in a punk bar on Saint-Denis. They were supposed to meet in Paris, where the band had a gig. But at the Gare du Nord Rebecca's luggage was stolen. She never found it, and followed her new girlfriend to Switzerland. Squatting was widespread in Switzerland at the time. For about ten years, Swiss law was astonishingly lax on the matter, and there were lots of squats. Rebecca turned to activism. She founded new squats, organized concerts, and even joined a Crass-inspired band, singing in German despite her imperfect command of the language. The songs were mashups of German avant-garde manifestos from the sixties, demanding kitsch, dirt, primordial mud, and desolation. After living together for three years, Rebecca and Hann broke up, but Rebecca stayed in Switzerland. She was evicted from her first squat and moved to a second and then a third, this time in Lausanne. The laws were becoming more restrictive. Her friends were getting older, too. Many of the squatters she had known in the early 2000s were sick or had died of overdoses, while others had found apartments, and jobs to pay for them. Rebecca never thought about coming back, and she felt no nostalgia about Yamachiche. Sometimes she felt a vague desire to write again, but she never acted on it. In November 2010 she moved to Spain, to an anarchist commune in the countryside not far from Tarragona. That was where she got sick, felled by a dysfunctional immune system. She thought back to Claire, to *Riot Inside*. Her disease dragged on for years, weakening her without ever quite convincing her to change her lifestyle or return to Quebec. She's still alive, but she looks at least fifteen years older than her age. She takes part in literary soirées where she recites Beckett, Cahun, and Burroughs. One evening she recalled some snatches of her brother's work—an excerpt from *Where the Murmurs Die*, she thought, or maybe *Years of Darkness*—and whispered a few sentences into the microphone.

Maxime Beauchemin started writing under the influence of Paul and Rebecca Deraps. He was born in Yamachiche, but he was a few years younger than the Deraps and he'd lived away from the village a few years, on the chemin du Canton-Nord, which runs alongside the Yamachiche River as it meanders through the fields before flooding into the marsh at the mouth, where the river opens up into Lac Saint-Pierre. As a child, Maxime was afflicted with epilepsy. His seizures became more frequent over the years, and left scars. As a teenager, he was a regular at the public library, like Paul Deraps. Both had similar literary tastes at similar stages, although Maxime preferred intergalactic science fiction novels to the medieval fantasy sagas Paul liked. As a young adult, Maxime had worked in a pork-processing plant where the 138 met the chemin du Canton-Nord, but he had to give it up when his epilepsy got worse. He lived alone above a convenience store in Yamachiche from the age of nineteen to twenty-four, when his parents wanted to move to Trois-Rivières into a more modern apartment with a view of the river, and gave him their house. Paul had just died, mowed down on the 138. After his death, Paul's parents had disposed of his belongings. A neighbour took the computer, and when he upgraded to a more recent machine two years later, he gave the old Compaq to Maxime. In a file called *The Calm Before the Calm*, Maxime found *The Time of the Dog*, *Where the Murmurs Die*, *Years of Darkness*, and other unfinished works by Paul Deraps. No one had looked at any of it since his death, or deleted a thing. Maxime read the sketches and drafts, fascinated.

Maxime lived alone. His evenings were long and he didn't have any hobbies, so he read Deraps' prose, appropriating it, gradually. The stories reflected his life back at him—his profound suffering, the feeling of being incomplete, his apparent inability to succeed in life, the constraints of living with a chronic disease, and the impression of always moving backwards. Since he'd lost his job and moved into the house on the chemin du Canton-Nord, his social life, such as it was, was limited to Chez Archie, the diner where he went to eat almost every day. Usually a cheeseburger, sometimes fish and chips or the daily special. He always sat in the same spot (over the years his belly grew bigger and he found it harder to squeeze behind the table) and ate in silence. After he came across Paul Deraps' writing, however, he started talking to other regulars. He was astounded to find out that no one had known that Deraps had been writing at all. Luc Lampron, who'd known Paul, told Maxime about a piece written by Deraps' sister and gave him his only copy of *Riot Inside*, which he'd kept since a crazy, unforgettable night in Montreal almost fifteen years earlier. Maxime recognized his own rage in Rebecca's work, and that was when he began to write.

Like Rebecca Deraps, Maxime Beauchemin authored a single work, but it was monstrous. Maxime wrote pages and pages by hand, an impulsive monologue, drawing on Paul and Rebecca's writing, feeding on it as if it were garbage. The syntax was faulty and the narrative structure repetitive and almost nonexistent, and Maxime borrowed the Deraps' vocabulary but only half understood the meaning of the words, mostly by intuition. For nearly three years he threw himself into writing. He wrote every day, driven by instinct, pouring out a monomaniacal text that eventually amounted to over a thousand pages. He mixed autobiographical sections about his experience with epilepsy and his interpersonal woes with fiction, inspired by childhood fairy tales, words and images from Paul and Rebecca's work, as well as the intergalactic series he'd read as a teenager.

Every morning, he went down to the basement and stored the previous day's output in a box next to *Riot Inside* and Paul's drafts, which he had printed before the old computer stopped working. Then he would head up and get back to work. In the basement, his words got damp; they mouldered. His prose was thoroughly misanthropic, misogyny jumbled with a general abhorrence of the human race. The hatred of the system in Rebecca's work was in Maxime's devoid of any emancipatory sweep, and the gruesome elements inspired by his adolescent reading picked at Paul's Beckettian and Kafkaesque imaginings. To be honest, Maxime's text was contemptible, virtually unreadable. So it was no great loss when the abundant snowfall of the winter of 2017 was followed by torrential rains in the spring, and their compound action caused the river to overrun its banks as it rarely had before. The fields were flooded, forcing burrowing animals out of the ground and up onto the road, where many of them ended up as Paul had. Water rushed into the basement of the small house on the chemin du Canton-Nord and soaked the boxes full of paper, rendering Deraps' and Maxime's work illegible. Maxime finally threw it all out, a gesture that felt definitive somehow, symbolic. He never wrote again.

There's probably no need to recount the rest of a life of sickness, loneliness, and mediocrity. But sometimes, as I look out over the Yamachiche River as it swells with brown water seeping from the fields, I think it must also hold some of the ink spilled by Paul, Rebecca, and Maxime, and I imagine the churnings of a literary scene, the closest that Yamachiche could ever get to one.

CITY WITHIN

BENEATH MONTREAL'S UNDERGROUND CITY is another, hollow and with endless storeys. I discovered the entrance by chance, and I head down there almost every night after work, closing the door behind me. Innumerable passageways connect rooms that are for the most part empty and uninhabited. Several intersect or follow each other—in the eighth subbasement, there are six parallel hallways—with openings that pass from one to the next, though they don't really seem designed to lead anywhere in particular. Most of the floors are connected by trapdoors, which you can slip through, though if you fall you're likely to get hurt. You can reach some of the traps by scaling pyramids made from furniture and planks. I stacked some for this very purpose, inspired by pre-existing structures.

Staircases are pretty rare. I know there are some that span several floors, though it's impossible to actually access any of them, until a door might open five or six landings down. Obviously exploring floors that appear at first to be completely cloistered becomes a fixation.

Over the course of several visits, I finally found a way to get to every floor except the third, which is still impenetrable: I couldn't find a door or a trapdoor to get in. When I climb up a staircase that crosses the third floor, and I bang against the wall, I can hear an echo behind it, though whether it's accessible or whether there is only an enclosed, unreachable space, I don't know.

The fourth subbasement has particularly low ceilings. You have to get around on your hands and knees, sometimes even crawling. The rooms there, on the other hand, are vast, wide expanses through which I inch along, dragging myself across the floor with my elbows or on my stomach.

In the sixth subbasement, the ceilings are surprisingly high—you'd have to be three times my height to touch them—and several corridors are so narrow that I shuffle sideways with my head turned so my shoulders don't rub against the walls. A door opens onto a spacious room bathed in pale light, the source of which remains invisible and mysterious. I once saw paw prints there, in the dust—a cat, but I never saw the animal. One night in December, as I was walking through the seventh subbasement, I heard a meowing sound that seemed to be coming from the ceiling. I tried to get to the cat but couldn't.

My explorations can be dangerous. I carry a bag with a rope, a water bottle, and some snacks, and I keep my flashlight handy. I don't always need it: several rooms and corridors are lit by lamps dangling from the ceiling, which I figure must be connected to the electrical grid of the outer city. Or skylights filter the glow from higher levels. There's also an entire floor, the eleventh, where to my knowledge there is not a single light. I find my way with my flashlight, or sometimes I deliberately just grope my way along. The game of blindness. It is completely dark. I step slowly, carefully, to avoid tumbling down stairs or through a hatch. The game goes on until I click on my flashlight again, often in a place that looks different than what I'd imagined. Then I'm off again to explore other floors.

In remote parts of the fifth subbasement, water dribbles down the walls. Some rooms are flooded, and I paddle across on rafts cobbled from pieces of shelves, tables, and chairs that I nail or tie together. A projector shines a white rectangle on a wall but no film flickers. Most of the rooms in the underground city are empty, but some have furniture, evidence of more or less recent occupation. In one, in the eighth or maybe the ninth subbasement, I once found a bathtub, full. The water was warm, almost hot, and I slid in. Somewhere farther along I could hear water falling drop by drop and, elsewhere, an almost inaudible squeak. I closed my eyes and I dropped my head under the surface, with only my lips and my nose above. I breathed slowly as the city radiated out around me, the rooms I imagined repeating endlessly, with me at the centre. I got out of the tub and dried myself, using my T-shirt as a towel, and walked outside.

I never saw the bathtub again. There are several rooms I've been to—often, even—without being able to find my way back. In one hallway I must have walked down a hundred times, last summer I saw a door I didn't know existed. When I tried to open it, it was locked, but two nights later, when I passed it again, it was open. Behind the door, a staircase led to the floor above, stopping at a wall. I panicked at the dead end, and bolted back down the stairs and through the open door, in the grasp of a fear, most likely irrational, that the door would close and I'd be left alone, hungry and thirsty in the stairwell, to curl up slowly in the dust.

Although I'm sometimes afraid of getting lost in all the rooms and hallways, or of becoming claustrophobic, that's never stopped me trying to get in. Over time I've created a map of landmarks and arranged the premises to make things easier—I tied a rope at the top of a shaft so I can slide down without falling, and I chalk markings on the walls—crosses, arrows, and circles to help me find my way around. I've also gotten into the habit of drawing half-plans, outlines of rooms, stairwells, and hallways, their proportions imperfect. When I see them again, they never seem to correspond exactly to the architecture of the place, and so I sometimes go back and adjust, erasing or colouring in the initial diagram in pink or yellow chalk over my white lines. I'm not sure—I'm not sure of much of anything about this labyrinthine underground—but sometimes, when I look at these drawings, I think others have altered or completed them, contours filled in for rooms I don't remember visiting. The length of a corridor surprises me. The cartography seems suddenly new, suspicious.

I don't know anything about the origin of the maze and, after venturing through it for months, I have no clue as to what it might have been—the whimsical project of a billionaire architect, or maybe an enormous atomic shelter—but everything down here is a study in uselessness: this is not a place made for living. The rooms and hallways don't seem to be arranged according to any logic, or at least none that I can discern. The scraps and the few pieces of furniture that are still in good shape give the impression that someone has lived here, but they could also be objects dragged in by other visitors before me, who might have chosen to live here for a time before going back to the outside. When I first heard a pounding pulse between the walls as I walked in a darkened hallway in the eleventh subbasement, a noise like someone running, the sign of a human presence, I wondered why they were running away from me, how I could possibly be a threat. A slow fear shivered through me. That night I came home earlier than usual, but my return to the surface seemed to take an especially long time. I paused, often. I stopped to listen. Nothing suggested that anyone else was there.

Other than the silence and the walking, and the pleasure of exploration, what I appreciate most in this underground city are the sounds. The reverberations of my footsteps. My breathing. The creak of the hinges when a door opens. The water weeping in. A pebble tossed against a wall resonating from room to room. I like hearing my voice. I let out a sigh as I walk down the halls, and the rustle of my breath repeats. Later, sitting against a wall, I catch myself talking. I wander back to childhood, that summer by a lake in the Eastern Townships, not far from the border, my body stretched out under the ferns. Diving from the rocks, the strangeness in the deep, black water full of bass and crayfish. Or I picture the rush of life above me, all the people downtown, the crowded streets. I get up, I go back to the outside. By the time I come out I'm always exhausted; I haven't slept. When I get to my apartment on Park, it's already light out. My cat wriggles over to purr on my belly as I fall asleep. In my dreams I'm back in the underground city again. The corridors stretch out even longer than in real life. For a long time I swim through the flooded halls. Sometimes

I meet a woman there, Camille. She is sitting against a wall in a far room. Her hood is pulled over her head, and its shadow hides her face, but I think I can make out features that look reptilian. Her tongue whips and whistles. My own skin, my belly, is dry and scaly, like it's been sunburned or like I have some disease, and I don't know how to get out of the underground. I wake up drenched in sweat, and I swear I won't go exploring again. Already it's time to go back to work: I lock myself in my office and for six hours I type in the subtitles of TV series and animal documentaries. My eyelids droop, and it's all I can do to keep my eyes open. But when I finish work, I go back to the underground city, as I do every night.

Sometimes I sleep down here. I curl up in a ball in a room, my jacket folded up under my head. The hallways stretch out around me. I breathe peacefully. The air is fresh. The room I've chosen isn't too dusty, and it's dimly lit. In a dream, I see Camille again. She looks at me as I sleep. She smiles at me. There's something tender about her, which she never shows in real life. I tear myself out of my dreams; I'm slow to get going. I turn down a hallway that seems to go on forever, and I want to sleep again. A door to my right is ajar. Camille is here, this time while I'm awake. She's huddled against a wall, and I sit less than a metre away, without touching her. In the gloom I can hardly see her eyes. I don't quite know why but they seem hostile, and I feel guilty even though I haven't done anything. There's no reason for her to hate me.

I'd been exploring the city for weeks before I met her for the first time. As I crawled through a narrow, low-ceilinged corridor, she was coming in the opposite direction. We were still, our heads a few centimetres apart. She stared at me without saying anything until I began to squirm back as she edged forward. When we were both finally somewhere we could stand, in an open space that seemed too large, she left immediately without saying a word. A few days later I saw her floating on a raft in a wide, flooded room. She didn't come close or try to talk to me, just poled away. Then one evening I found her sleeping in the corner of a room, her hood pulled over her head on the concrete floor. I lay down next to her. When she woke up she said, *This place is mine, Rocco. Have you forgotten?* My name is Pascal, and I've never met a Rocco, but I answered, *No. I've never forgotten, Camille.* She lay down next to me—a rare thing—and put her head on my lap. I smelled her, felt the warmth of her body, her heart beating. I wanted to kiss her.

I suspect she goes outside as little as possible. Every time I see her now I give her food, usually a sandwich I've made her. She never thanks me, but she swallows the meal hungrily. In one room, on a table, I once found some leftovers in a styrofoam container—some rice, chicken bones, a bit of salad. I imagined a theft, a quick in-and-out, higher up, up in the underground restaurants of Place Ville Marie.

I haven't seen Camille for over a month. There's no sign of her in any room, hallway, or staircase. I saw the cat's tracks again without seeing the cat. Every night, I dream of the underground city as I lie between its walls. One night, I dreamed that the whole grid was nestled in the body of a giant automaton. Another time, the city sank so deep it seemed to plummet through the earth. I thought I'd never see Camille again, but more and more she filled my dreams. She had the face of a cat, an eel, a shrew. Her arms were coiled; my own limbs were evaporating. When I finally came across her outside my dreams, she was crouching in the middle of a room, urine puddling beneath her. I turned my head away. *I know these hallways by heart,* she said abruptly. *Everything here belongs to me.* I didn't know what to say. I just wanted to stay near her.

At work my boss told me that I didn't look so hot, I needed to pull myself together, I wasn't sleeping enough. I nodded but still I continued exploring the secret city.

Today, the entrance, the only door I know of, is marked with a sign I drew, a miniature, stylized representation of a labyrinth. I pulled the door shut behind me, leaving the symbol for others, and I've never gone back up. Now that I live in the underground city, now that I sleep and dream here, it burrows into my body, too, into my head, letting me communicate with Camille—withdrawing into this shared solitude where I lose her and must find her again constantly. Where we live not outside of the world but in the real.

THE FOREST AND THE CITY

FOR A LONG TIME I used to like wandering around in the woods. I don't go there anymore. I tramped along on slippery, unpredictable terrain, plagued by mosquitoes droning around my head. My boots sank into the peat and the humus as I avoided the roots. Sometimes I found abandoned cans or the rusty shell casings of hunters near the droppings of invisible animals lurking in the mud or in snarled hollows.

I kept my eyes down, watching the ground. I scanned the base of fir trees, the birches and larches where strange mushrooms grow, stems jammed in the ground or bubbling on dead wood. Some of them have no shape, they look like a bulge or a cancerous growth. Others are long and smooth, elegantly white. The most beautiful are often the most dangerous: nature is a hypocrite, captivating in order to capture. I've read about it in field guides. *Amanita phalloides*, the death cap, causes agony for hours. An unwitting hiker's body ends up being consumed by animals.

Back then my wife was into mushrooms. She wandered off the path, and I followed, deking between the branches as they whipped at our faces. Boletes covered with spines rose up from the soil. Their flesh is often eaten by worms. The russulas spread their reddish caps. The whiteness of *Amanita virosa*, destroying angel, seemed surreal against the brownish carpet of the forest. My wife used to pick chanterelles, milk caps, waxy caps, and wood mushrooms and collect them in her basket. She'd never eaten a poisonous mushroom, but sometimes she would touch one to her tongue to find out what it tasted like. I never put them near my mouth, I didn't even touch them. Each time my wife insisted, but I didn't taste any of the mushrooms we brought back. They seemed too close to the damp earth, the darkness of the woods, animals hidden beneath the fallen leaves, they seemed to be about getting lost, and I hoped for the end of the season, when the forest was returned to the hunters, and then winter, when we would stop foraging under the ferns.

There was one wet spring in particular. For the last time, I followed my wife into the woods. It was drizzling. The mosquitoes hadn't woken up yet. Patches of snow lingered here and there beneath the trees. I didn't know how long the animals had been awake since the end of the winter, but they must have been hungry, sniffing the earth in search of the bodies of those who hadn't yet reopened their springtime eyes and on whose carcass some scraps of lean flesh remained, trapped between hide and bone, waiting to be eaten. The cool air went right through my jacket. My wife and I hardly spoke. A curl of breath rose from my mouth. A few birds were beginning to sing. When my wife told me she was leaving me, I wasn't surprised. I headed back with her. We were deep in the forest, and the road was over an hour's hike away. We were walking together, but already I felt a frightening solitude, the coldness of nights alone, the kind of loneliness that wakes you and doesn't let you go back to sleep.

We met a few times. We talked about keeping in touch, but our lives drifted in opposite directions. I stopped going to the forest; I went deeper into the city. Now I work at night in the metro stations, in maintenance. After the metro closes, a few of us walk along the platforms. I go into empty cars, I lift trapdoors, I make sure all the mechanical stuff is working.

In winter, I get home before sunrise; in summer, shortly after dawn. I open my door on Jarvis. Before I go to sleep, I read for a while, usually detective novels, true crime, or war stories. I read until my eyes close and the book slips out of my hands. Words and images from my bedtime stories often contaminate my dreams: frantic chases under trees, men slithering along in the mud to slit the enemy's throat, torn-up bodies at the bottom of a pond.

Once I read a transcript of the interrogation of a serial killer. He'd abandoned his victims in the woods. He recounted a night spent dragging a body through the undergrowth, looking for the best place to put it in the ground, but he couldn't make up his mind about the ideal spot to make it disappear. He had finally settled on something at dawn, terrified at the idea of daybreak, and buried the body only a few metres from the road, in a much shallower grave than he'd have liked. In spite of all that, he marvelled, it had taken more than twenty years to find the remains. That night

I dreamed of a corpse rotting deep in the woods. Mushrooms had sprouted on the skin and pushed through the clothes to find the light. They covered the whole body: feet, legs, belly, chest, arms, head. There were even mushrooms growing out of the eyes. When I woke up, the whole day had gone by and it was night again. I took a long, hot shower and masturbated under the streaming water without really enjoying it. The next day was garbage day. A couple of years earlier I'd read the confessions of another killer, from the Chicago suburbs. He used to put the dismembered bodies of his victims in Glad bags; he thought that was the strongest brand. He never took the bags out the night before the garbage truck came, waiting until morning for fear that rats, squirrels, or alley cats might come and tear them open during the night. Most of the time he only put them out on the street when he heard the garbage truck approaching. He was afraid too that homeless people would open the bags searching for cans or food. But his bags got mixed up with the others. Trash with other trash, he said, rot with rot.

That evening in July I remembered his words as I walked out of my apartment carrying my garbage bins. The trash was piling up on the sidewalk. The garbage strike was dragging on and on, and in the muggy heat the stench was horrible. Despite the heat wave I slept with the windows closed. I'd decided a few days before to buy an air conditioner. It spat the hot air outside and its whirr rocked me to sleep. In the street, at the height of summer, the air sticks to your skin day and night. I can't imagine the heat in larger cities or in countries farther south, let alone in those immense, sprawling megacities where the population increases by hundreds of thousands every year. A guy I work with, Will, says they're like tumours. They're growing constantly, developing without any kind of urban planning, gradually parasitizing the planet, absorbing other towns and villages, swallowing up forests and farmland, paving over rivers and blasting through hills. Imagine crossing Beijing, the hundreds of kilometres of the city, twenty million people, pushing through randomly, looking for a way out... Then, after walking for hours, you arrive, exhausted, at the rice paddies billowing out as far as the eye can see.

That's what we often tell ourselves, Will and I: there's no way out.

He was born in Long Lake, a reserve in Northern Ontario, more than a thousand kilometres from here. He loved the forest, he tells me, but he hasn't been back in years. He tells me about the litter-strewn mud by the creek, families growing up too fast, rape and incest, girls perpetually pregnant, the woods, where over the years he lost his way. Now he's afraid he would actually get lost. He doesn't know if he wants to go back.

We work at night, underneath the city. We rarely see daylight. We talk about the forest and about the city, which feel foreign to us and are hard to love. With Will I grease the gears, I make sure the bolts are right and everything is running as it should. The fatigue catches up to us by the end of the night. We head up together in the early morning before going our separate ways. A pale glow rises between the skyscrapers as I return home. The truck still hasn't come by and soon the trash will be smouldering and seeping in the sun. I close my eyes as I walk. I imagine mushrooms growing here among the bags of garbage, their long, white shapes, their caps gleaming in the morning light—the reflection of the strange hostility of what might be real as they take root in the filth. The ground is suddenly unsteady under my feet. I take a few faltering steps and open my eyes—I don't want to fall—and I think back to the decaying bodies vanishing into the degrading forest floor.

THE LANGUAGE OF HUNTERS

I HEARD THE CAWS and the blatter of the crows taking flight before I saw the bear, its carcass resting on a bed of sphagnum moss. The birds had pried their beaks into the open wound on the animal's head. The blood had long since dried, but their persistent digging had exposed the whitish mud inside his skull. A forest ranger once told me that animal remains disappear quickly. Insects and animals of all kinds eat them, usually in a single night, until there's nothing left—a few bones, scattered and almost invisible among the dry branches and leaves on the forest floor.

It was the first time I had ever seen a bear up close. A couple of times I had caught a glimpse of one on the road, mostly farther north in the Mauricie. Never on my countless walks through the woods around our family cottage had I even supposed I might come across a bear. It was a sunny afternoon in early September. The forest was still green, though a few rare leaves were starting to turn, their yellow heralding the arrival of fall. Hunting season hadn't opened yet. The bear had been shot by a human weapon, which worried me. I remembered my father telling me not to go into the forest from mid-September; it no longer belonged to us, it was the hunters'. My father used to hunt—a bit of everything, deer, moose, caribou, coyotes, bears—but he had put his gun away and felt that we should be wary of those who used them: men unmoving, flat on the ground for hours waiting for a chance to pull the trigger. I could hear his voice, and I remembered his hair, which was thick and black until the end of his life. Like me, he loved walking alone in the forest. I had come by him there once unexpect-edly, under the fir trees, among the ferns. The branches were dense, filtering the sun. We were far from the road, in the dense coniferous edge of a bog, and running into my father there was unsettling, unnatural. His presence seemed for-eign. We had walked back to the cottage barely speaking, uncomfortable in the intimacy of the undergrowth.

That day in September, boots planted in the red and green moss, the animal body brought me back to my father as I heard the rasp of the crows ratcheting in my head. They were crying out for their meal. They wanted me to leave so they could continue eating the bear, but I stood my ground. A cool wind shuffled through the branches. Flies were congested on the coagulated blood and around the visible brain of the animal. Some circled around me, resting on my head. Above me the crows flapped their wings. I imagined foxes, weasels, fishers, maybe even coyotes coming to join the feast. I opened my mouth. I let out a cry, as if to announce, *I am here*. I called three times, addressing both man and beast. I thought of the hunters' guns. I felt like I couldn't leave, like I wanted to dig a grave for the bear or take it with me, gut it, cut through its flesh, remove its animal skin and put it on. The hunter hadn't bothered to take the fur or the meat, and I wondered why we taxidermied animals but not humans, why we tried to preserve animals in some approximation of life but hid the bodies of our loved ones until we forgot about them, until there was nothing left.

I pictured an exhibition of stuffed bodies, my mother, my father, my grandmother, my grandfather, and those who had gone before them standing frozen in the corner of my apartment or at the cottage, decorative. I imagined dozens of stuffed, posed bodies, several generations of ancestors, the faces of some recalling others: the continuity of family and the constant presence of death, the embodiment of mortality. I told myself it was better to hide death, to bury it and overwhelm it with a heavy stone, hard to move. My father's blown-out skull would have thwarted any effort at preservation, unless he'd been made into a monster, a thing without a face or a head.

I was the one who had found his body that day in October the previous year. I hadn't heard from him for a long time. I hardly ever saw him. My mother had died two years earlier, of a heart attack. A few days before my father's death I called him and got his answering machine. I heard his voice, and I recorded my own. *Hi, it's me. I hope you're okay. I was hoping to go up to the cottage this weekend. Is it available?* He didn't call back. I called him again the next day. Again, no answer. I needed some time alone. My work as a teacher was weighing on me, and my words were empty. I felt like everything I said was pointless. I left Montreal on the 40, driving east. At Louiseville, I headed north. A bit before Saint-Alexis-des-Monts, I turned onto a gravel road and into the woods.

My father had taken out his old shotgun. I didn't know he had it still. I don't know how many animals he'd killed with it when he was hunting. It was a large-calibre Remington rifle. He had it attached to a chair. He had knelt down and placed his mouth around the barrel. It must have been cold on his lips. And he must have pushed down almost to his throat and squeezed it tight between his teeth, because his mouth was still resting on the gun. Blood, bone, and brains had sprayed out behind it, staining his jacket and the floor.

When I found his body, I froze at the horror of the scene. I couldn't make sense of it. Nor did I ever, really; I've never understood. My father didn't leave me a letter. I had never seen him write. He was a man of few words, a man of silence. And I didn't know how to read his death: his mouth on the gun, the brains and blood. I went out. I left him at the cottage. I drove through the woods, my phone wasn't getting a signal. When I got close to the 349, I dialled 911 and waited for the ambulance.

Now, a year later, the crows were circling over my head and I left them the bear, I left it to the birds and the insects and whatever other critters would make short work of it, erase any trace of its existence. I let out another cry as I headed under the trees. This time I didn't just call out to warn animals and hunters, but to break the quiet as the cawing behind me waned.

I walked quickly to the gravel path that leads to the cottage. The sky was a searing blue. Sweat soaked my chest as I climbed up the hillside. Animals were probably spying on me from the underbrush—foxes, partridges, maybe a young bear attracted by the meat, driven by its predatory instincts, the urge to devour the carcass of the other beast slaughtered in the forest. I wished this imaginary bear good luck, I hoped it would stay away from men and escape the hunters. I imagined what its life would be like, in the bush, a life among the ferns. Nights alone on the moss and leaves.

That night in September, I slept at the cottage. Despite my father's suicide, the blood that still stained the floor, I'd stayed here now and again since his death. Naturally everyone told me not to, but I loved the woods. I had repainted the walls, I had changed the furniture and the dishes. I had thrown away my parents' old clothes. The sheets they had slept on, too. I burned my childhood photo album. Erased. I wanted to forget, and I wanted solitude under the trees, the fresh air, the smell of the peat.

Erase. Yet I could hardly sleep. That night, when I finally drifted off, I saw myself lying in the shade of the undergrowth on a bed of sphagnum moss. Blood flowed from my skull. My mouth was dry. I couldn't breathe. Above me I could see the glare of the sun. Crows, shrews, and ants pushed into my sacrificed body. I was in pain, unable to die and find out the secret of my father's death.

Today, as I talk again to students, as my words seem empty again, I think of the punctured skull, the flat gaze. I think of a hunter I ran into once on the gravel path, and I imagine knowing an ancient language made of shards of bone and drops of blood, plunging my fingers into the substance discharged from my father's head to decipher a message etched there. I swallow. I long for the aloneness of the cottage.

Throughout the fall I go back every week. More and more often I hear the hunters' gunshots. I feel like going into the forest, I imagine myself dressed in my father's skin, but I rarely stray from the path. Like the bear, I hope for colder days, the salvation of winter and then, after hibernation, a new awakening, heading out again among the ferns, walking in other footsteps, not knowing whether I might find him along the way.

THE WORLD BEYOND

SAMUEL DIDN'T EXPRESS HIMSELF the same way after his stroke. His mouth found it hard to shape sounds. His sentences were cryptic, his syntax faulty. He inverted the meaning of words and invented new ones that only he could understand.

At the time, he had just broken up with his wife. He had no children, and few friends. Making friends had never been easy for him. He was on good terms with his colleagues in comparative literature at the University of Montreal. He met some of them for a drink now and again, but the relationships never went beyond intellectual conversations.

To tell the truth, what Samuel enjoyed more than anything was reading and analyzing texts.

He had a passion for the most abstruse verse, for poems that deconstructed language or claimed to destroy it. Samuel loved Russian literature and cinema, and had once written a hundred-page essay on a single poem by Khlebnikov. *Construction and Destruction of Language* earned him the respect of his peers, although no one read the essay in its entirety.

During his convalescence, a couple of colleagues and thesis students visited him a few times. His ex-wife never came. Friends he hadn't seen for over a year brought him flowers. His sister Dolores, who lived in Los Angeles, where she worked in the pharmaceutical industry, spent the first week with him. After that, she came less often.

Samuel's rehabilitation was slow. Each day, when nurses, doctors, or occupational therapists spoke to him, he answered in a changed, aphasic language that he thought made sense. But Samuel seemed to be talking only to himself. Signifiers had changed. A chair was called *legs,* his work was the *tower,* his first name was *Victim,* his favourite author was *The Hangman.* Samuel mixed up letters and merged words without even realizing he was creating new ones. Reading was difficult. He deciphered texts slowly, reconstructing the meaning of sentences as if he were a child. And his memory was fickle. He thought he was born in February, but actually his birthday was in September. He forgot the name of Victoriaville, where he had grown up. He'd been married three times, he thought, but then he wasn't sure he had ever married at all.

Yet he ended up reconstructing his memory and learning to read and to speak again. It took him months: his adult head and his aging neurons weren't used to gathering knowledge as children do. As he learned, he was surprised to find an almost intellectual pleasure in rediscovering language and, through language, of renegotiating his relationship to reality. *The brain is an amazing machine*, Dr. Liu, the neurologist in charge of his case, liked to say, and although gaps remained, including some memory loss (Samuel had forgotten his honeymoon, he couldn't remember the subject of his master's thesis) and muddled language (he confused *peach* and *plum*, and *bladder* and *Burlyuk*—one of his favourite authors), his state came close to what is referred to as normal.

When he came home in February, four months after his stroke, Samuel doubted that he was fully recovered. He suspected he was leaving a part of himself behind. Something inside him was misshapen, as if all his life he'd been kept upright by a rod, and now it was bent. He also felt like he was stepping into a deep solitude, more cavernous and lonely than he had ever known; it had to do with all that time in the hospital and in rehab, and with the impression of having spoken a language that didn't correspond to life, as if it served to describe a parallel universe, an almost imaginary space out of step with reality.

Samuel wasn't cleared to resume his work at the university yet; he needed to rest. So he stayed home. His house was unnecessarily large. It had already been too big when he was married, and now the space seemed all the more superfluous. His habits changed, too: he varied his meals very little, content with three or four recipes. He stopped watching films online, while before, for a long time, he'd been fascinated by Vertov and Tarkovsky, and he didn't turn on the television because the images exhausted him. He only left his house to go to the grocery store, and he was never gone for long. He spent his days between his bedroom, the kitchen, and the living room. He had started to read and write again. He wasn't writing academic articles and essays, but autobiographical, fragmentary fiction about the experience of his illness—the proximity of death at the moment of the stroke, being alone in an outside reality, forging new paths at the risk of getting lost. He no longer wanted to write on a computer, and the coffee table in the living room was cluttered with sheets he'd scratched up by hand.

His writings drifted gradually, dealing with the subject of the disease more indirectly. The transformation was progressive: the scenes he wrote no longer evoked his suffering or the moment of the stroke. Words like *ambulance*, *catheter*, and *convalescence* disappeared; their universe represented reality less faithfully now. He stopped writing in the first person, but instead made up fictional narrators.

His characters moved through a large hospital. The white walls were perpetually dirty, and the same fluorescent lights sizzled in each corridor. The stairs led to nearly identical floors, with only a few details to tell them apart—a still life hanging on the wall, a bed undone. Lit signs blared *EXIT* and led to other rooms and hallways, none of which allowed people to leave the hospital. The hospital had been built on muddy, marshy grounds, and the basement was damp, with water seeping in. Those who ventured into

69

the basement might take several hours to reach the upper floors, and then walked around in circles. From page to page, Samuel's characters were framed by the same filthy walls, the same crackling lights, the same empty rooms. Little by little, they were overcome by fear and fatigue. Little by little, it seemed that reality was altered: the walls flowed as if they were liquid, the ceiling bulged, feet left marks in the floor like clay. Then his characters would hide in a laboratory, a storeroom, or a palliative care ward. Together, they tried to reassure each other, but they spoke words they didn't remember knowing, and the others misunderstood, as if each person were speaking a foreign language. In the hope of being understood, they wrote on the walls, in the dust, or they repeated the words, heard them echo, made drawings to try to show what they were saying. In Samuel's stories, people created a common language, a language reinvented. They renamed the walls and the doors, which were sometimes also opened by words. They uttered words that changed the appearance of rooms, widened them, stretched them, broke openings in the walls. They spoke words that made staircases unfurl. They created possible exits from the hospital, doors on the outside walls and ladders unfolding from its windows, trapdoors unlatched from the basement ceiling. From one story to the next, their wandering seemed never to end, though it was like they were escaping from reality, visiting a reality other than their own, stranger to it, and in which they sometimes thought they were still confined, but they always ended up finding the real world beyond. Always they sank in the middle of the marsh until Samuel returned them to the hospital, reinventing the halls and rooms.

He wrote these fictions for days on end, devoting himself to the work with an energy he hadn't had for a long time. He was lost in the stories. He had no appetite and did nothing but write. Samuel never reread his stories. His approach, if you can call it that, was repetition: running into the same walls, turning down the same hallways at the same corners, but each time slightly off course. He didn't notice it right away, but over time he stopped choosing his words the same way, inverting meaning or ascribing meanings known only to him. He no longer used *wall*, *hallway*, or *clay*; rather *wood*, *right*, or *entangled*—not as if they were synonyms, but to say something else, to fill the holes in language, describe the world differently. After two weeks, a first neologism appeared in his sentences, and then many more. It was like a new language was slowly parasitizing his own. Soon some of Samuel's sentences would have been indecipherable to anyone else. It was doubtful whether he himself could read them. Long passages seemed to be made up of a composite language, seemingly formed by an amalgam of distinct idioms, while others seemed to want to shuck off any human sounds. As the days went by, Samuel had the feeling that his language was decomposing, and at the same time he was sure that this new language could capture the nuances of his life better than any other.

The fatigue would hit after he'd been writing for hours, and suddenly he would have a terrible headache. He collapsed on his bed and slept for hours. When he woke, he never remembered his dreams. It took Samuel a long time to get up, but when he finally came down to the living room, he started writing again.

After three months of writing, one day he woke up lying at the foot of his bed. It was hard to get up. His head ached unbearably. The real world around him was covered with a whitish film. Again, he was afraid to die. He feared the loneliness associated with death, a deep, black

loneliness, without language and without anywhere to go. Outside it was already autumn.
Leaves brushed along the window's edge, and
fell, rotting in the gutters. When he called the
ambulance, he thought he was speaking a language other than his own, and was surprised
that he was understood. On the way to the hospital he was delirious, half conscious. When he
got there, a Haitian nurse told him the voices of
angels were speaking through him.

This time again the rehabilitation was lengthy,
but again the brain proved a miraculous thing,
and four months later Samuel was able to return
home. After his second recovery, he never wrote
again, he lost all desire to read or write. He got
in touch with old friends who hadn't heard from
him for a long time, and who didn't know anything about his illness. He flew to Los Angeles to
see his sister, and together they got drunker than
Samuel had since he was a teenager. (Samuel fell
asleep by the pool under a sky spilling over with
stars.) The friends with whom he reconnected
introduced him to a woman his age. She was a
museum curator. He found her attractive and her
intelligence pleased him, and they became lovers.

Those who knew him said he'd come back
to life. A former colleague even hinted that he

was more alive than before. But Samuel had left behind a dead man, and some days when he woke up it was so clear to him how opaque reality was: he was scrambling between thick walls that were closing in, his hands were clammy, his heart beat faster. He opened his mouth as if to speak but said nothing. Yet in his sleep he sometimes spoke a foreign tongue that said something else about his life. He could open doors with it; he would look for a way out.

POLAND

FIFTEEN YEARS BEFORE I WAS BORN, my mother had a son, her first. He left home early and hardly ever visited. We only lived together for the first few years of my life, and I don't have many memories of that time, though I remember his face clearly, large and broad, peering down at me in the cradle. I have another memory, too: one spring day, in the garden, he stepped on the end of a long earthworm stretching in the green grass and held it captive while the worm squirmed and bent its rings, unable to escape.

My brother left home shortly after he turned eighteen. He was going to the city, leaving Maskinongé for Montreal to study engineering. That year, he came back for Christmas. He had gained weight. His head seemed bigger too. I remember his laugh as he sat at the table with my father. Actually, I think they were drunk and my brother was laughing and whispering into our father's ear, as if he were telling him secrets.

That was the last time I saw him. He left Montreal soon after. He headed east on the 40 without stopping in Maskinongé, and followed the river beyond Quebec City. He went to Sept-Îles and found work at an aluminium plant, even though he hadn't finished school. My mother called him now and again. Their conversations were short. My brother had never been much of a talker, and didn't see any point in catching up. I could hear my mother ask him about the weather. In my child's mind, winters in Sept-Îles lasted forever. As the years went by, the phone calls became even less frequent, and then almost nonexistent. I found out much later that he'd left Sept-Îles. He'd gone even farther north, a thousand kilometres from Maskinongé, to settle in Aguanish, on the shores of the Saint Lawrence. Apparently he didn't have a job. He'd bought a house outside the village. When my father died on April 12, 2013, of throat cancer, my brother didn't come to the funeral. I was fifteen years old; my brother would have been thirty. A month later his first novel was published.

My mother went to Trois-Rivières to buy a copy. I don't know if she read it, but she cut out every one of the articles published about the book and pasted them in a scrapbook. She did the same for my brother's other novels.

The book was called *Poland*. It was the story of two brothers who lived together without friends or family on the banks of a river. Every morning the river shimmered in the sunshine. I say two brothers, but as the narrative went on, the distance between them seemed to dwindle, and they sometimes seemed to be one. Their bodies were thin. You could see their ribs sticking out as they ran along the shore. The novel was about a famine in a country without a name. The fields were dead and dry, and the river had no fish. All that was left to eat was what could be hunted. All the locals traipsed around the woods, farther and farther away, avoiding the tracks of others and searching for spots no one had ever been before, where there might possibly be more game. They were all swallowed up into the pine forests and the bogs, the landscape repeating itself as their feet sank into the moss and mud. After walking for several days, the brothers still hadn't killed any deer or partridge. They couldn't aim, they complained. It was as if hunger were blurring their sight. They were seeing double. Soon they ran out of ammunition. They gnawed at roots and ferns. One night by the light of the full moon they saw a bear in the bottom of a valley. The bear had no escape. The two pulled out their knives. At daybreak there was only one brother left, limping. His right arm was in a sling. His whole body was red. A cloud of flies hummed around him. He threw all the bones into the same pit, the bear's and his brother's. For days, wrapped in fur, he smoked the bear meat, wondering how he would carry so much by himself. The smoke rose toward the sky, drifting on the wind, and the scent attracted both men and animals. Some villagers caught up to the brother, but he didn't say a word, too suspicious of them to try to share. He kept his fur on and charged at them like a wild animal. In the middle of the night the bear's remains seemed enormous on his scrawny body. It was like the two brothers were living inside it—together they were invincible—but at dawn the remaining brother was dead on the forest floor, on the moss, where his corpse would decompose.

Of my brother's books, this is the only one I have read from start to finish. I don't know if I really enjoyed it. I think I read it mostly so I'd have something to say to him if he ever came back. I was living alone in Maskinongé with my mother. We subsisted on almost nothing. I didn't go out much, I read books by the dozen—any genre, any author, books that had piled up on our shelves, my father's books. My brother must have read those too. The summer was rainy. Clouds of mosquitoes descended upon me when I went out at dusk. I had few friends. I didn't know how to talk to girls. I rarely went far, riding my bike to the nearby convenience store to buy chips or pop. When I saw an issue of *National Geographic* about Poland on the top of a pile at a garage sale, I wondered why my brother had chosen that title for his book. I looked at the pictures. I wasn't sure I understood. I told myself that Poland must have looked like the North Shore or the Mauricie.

My brother's second book, *The Twilight Elephant*, was published a year later. I liked that title. I liked what the critics said, what I read in my mother's clippings or on the internet. The cover was split down the middle by a picture of an elephant's trunk. The novel was set in no man's land, a muddy field where shells scooped out craters, or graves. The only humans were cadavers. The place was populated by animals, which gathered in herds with no distinction between species, or for predator and prey. The war had lasted several generations. The no man's land seemed to be the whole world, and the animals couldn't agree on the name of the country they lived in: Poland, Congo, Ireland, Abkhazia, Kazakhstan? Legends were mixed up, and other myths were made up. The squirrel was voluble and eloquent and seemed to know everything. Above the pack rose the twilight elephant, a huge pachyderm that blocked out the sky, whose trunk could change the trajectory of the earth, and whose ears beat as if it were flying.

I don't know what else the book said, whether the elephant was a mirage or whether it actually existed. I've only read reviews, some excerpts online, and the descriptions on the back cover and on the publisher's website. Unlike the first novel, my mother hadn't bought the book (she almost never bought books), and the library didn't have it. But I was reading less anyway; I'd made a friend. Mathias and I spent our evenings drinking in the cemetery, along the river, or in the old hunting blind my father had built in an ash tree. Some evenings, too drunk to go home, we slept out in the cornfields or huddled among the trees. When we woke up and wandered around the countryside, we came across dead marmots or skunks in the ditches.

At first my mother worried, and she looked for me all the time. But then she got used to my absence, or maybe she didn't have the strength anymore. In any case, she was rarely at home. She worked cleaning houses or the motel in Louiseville. When she didn't have time to cook, we ate frozen pizza; anyway, I liked that better than what she made, which hadn't changed in years. I was a skinny teenager. I don't know if I was handsome. Later people told me I had nice eyes. When I sucked in my stomach it seemed to disappear, but I could chug litres of beer. Sometimes when Mathias and I were drinking, I told him stories. Thinking back, today, they might as well have been written by my brother. Stories about mud, about cat-men, dog-men, shrew-men, stories about Poland, the Mauricie, the North Shore. Stories about Nowhere, and without any chance of a future.

My brother's third and final book was like that. I didn't know right away that it had come out. My mother didn't tell me, and I didn't ask.

When I opened her scrapbook one warm summer afternoon, I saw new articles she had cut out, just a few, including a short piece from *Le Nord-Côtier*, a Sept-Îles weekly, which announced the book's release without commenting on it. But they'd printed a photo of my brother, sitting on the steps of an old plank house. He had a considerable gut spilling out from under his sweater. An impressive beard covered his face. The picture wasn't very good. I didn't really recognize his features, but despite our difference in size I thought he looked like me. I thought my head was large too. Macrocephaly: I repeated the word. It could have been one of his book titles.

His third book was his longest, almost six hundred pages. I was surprised he'd written it so fast, though what else did he have to do, in Aguanish, on the North Shore, with no sign that he had a girlfriend, friends, or any other occupation or activity? It was called *Bipeds*. The book got mixed reviews. Some insisted that it was a masterpiece. Others found it unpalatable and wondered why it had been published at all. Few people actually read it. There were innumerable characters, but they all had the same name. They travelled from town to town and stopped along the way in villages, all of which were called Maskinongé. All the characters had more than two legs—they walked on three, four or six limbs, they were tripeds, mammals or insects. Each one had a stomach ache. I had a hard time picturing any of it. The summer ended in Maskinongé. I had already decided to leave.

For years I continued to watch out for new books by my brother. I don't know if he was still writing, but nothing was ever published. I live in Montreal now, and I still remember the picture in the article my mother cut out, my brother's head and belly so big he somehow existed inside them. My own life is what's contained beneath his ribs, or inside his skull. Some evenings, I open up my computer, a file called Maskinongé. I write sentences, and every time I delete them. It's about an umbilical cord that looks like a worm, and also about my love for my brother—an irrational love, based on distance and failure, the feeling that we are both still prisoners of Maskinongé.

I haven't been back since my mother moved into a retirement home in Trois-Rivières. But I've never stopped living in the same Poland, the same North Shore, and the same Mauricie as my brother.

SUKHUMI

THE FIRST TIME I MET SPIROBERG IN A DREAM, I didn't know if he was dreaming about me or the other way around. He came to me in my sleep every night for months, and I was never sure who was dreaming of whom. Spiroberg was from the late nineteen-eighties; I was living in the second decade of the next millennium. I didn't know if I was dreaming about the past or whether he was dreaming about the future. We were in a liminal space between his life and mine.

At the time I was a research assistant at McGill University and working as a tour guide at the Redpath Museum. I led visitors among the skeletons and the taxidermied animals, explaining the feeding habits of the Japanese spider crab, the preservation of prehistoric deer antlers in the depths of Irish bogs, or the techniques the Egyptians had used to mummify cats, falcons, and ibises.

Spiroberg was a researcher at the Primate Institute of Experimental Pathology and Therapy in Sukhumi, also known as the Monkey Nursery. The Institute was where Professor Seminova had trained monkeys for space travel. It was also where Ilya Ivanov had tried to breed men and apes—using female chimpanzees and human sperm—before he was accused of associating with the international bourgeoisie. He was exiled to Kazakhstan and never returned. Hundreds of monkeys were kept in cages and pens in Sukhumi, in the foothills of the Caucasus less than a kilometre from the Black Sea.

In my dreams, I often found Spiroberg there, in Sukhumi. We walked on the beach—Sukhumi had been a popular Abkhaz seaside resort during the Soviet era. My friend and I would chat until dawn about the hierarchical structures of baboons and the genus Cercopithecus, the genetic proximity between humans and chimpanzees, the ability of monkeys to survive outside of their natural habitat. Other times we would stroll along the halls of the Redpath Museum, and

I described to Spiroberg the scientific progress of my contemporary world—mammalian cloning, genomic sequence correction, artificial intelligence, head transplant experiments... Sometimes we split off at the end of a hallway and ended up suddenly back in Sukhumi. Together we walked through the Institute, past caged macaques and mandrills, and sick animals or amputees, or we went out among the apes in the larger enclosure. The Caucasus Mountains loomed behind us, and the forest seemed to go on forever. When I woke up in my apartment in the McGill Ghetto, I had a surprisingly clear memory of my dreams: Spiroberg's face and our conversations, the wind off the Black Sea blowing through Sukhumi, the stink of the monkey droppings in the cages at the Institute. Other images floated back to me before fading away—primates fleeing among the bones and taxidermy at the Redpath, and others that followed me, as if I were being hunted. I didn't think about it much. I headed along Milton and down University. In class, I listened to my teachers go on about evolutionary genetics, molecular biology, and neurobiology, and then, in the evening, I found myself in Sukhumi again. Spiroberg was there, and the Institute primates, apes captured from the plains and jungles of Africa and transported in cages aboard ocean liners that crossed the Mediterranean then sailed up the Bosporus and over the Black Sea to Abkhazia. I could see the forests of the Caucasus behind them. I wanted to sink into the woods, to slip into the shadows. I was on the path alone, pushing through the trees, and popped out into a hallway, at McGill, with Spiroberg at my side once more.

We met like this for months, complicit, in a conjunction of dreams where we developed a close relationship based on mutual affinities, and I existed in Sukhumi as fully as I did in Montreal, I lived among the apes as in the university halls. When I talked with Spiroberg, I never once doubted that he understood me. It was as though we shared a brain, as if we were connected by invisible neurons. I slept more and longer, neglecting my classes; I liked my dreams better. The days were too long. I had no idea what was going on in the world. That summer, in 2016, there were attacks all over the place, an attempted coup in Turkey, forest fires raging in California and Colorado. In Montreal the expressway was paralyzed for a whole day when a tanker truck caught fire.

Time passed in Sukhumi too. Spiroberg seemed increasingly worried. He looked tired, he lost all interest in science and showed more affection for the monkeys, as if he were afraid of losing them. We no longer walked on the beach; we stayed at the Institute. It seemed like he was locking himself in. His gestures were spastic, and he wouldn't look me in the eye. When he came to the Redpath Museum with me, we would see monkeys sitting on the railings or hanging out in the prehistoric rib cage of the *Gorgosaurus libratus,* sheltering there, escaping from Spiroberg's reality to mine. In Abkhazia, where he lived, it was already the beginning of the nineties. Armed militias roved through Sukhumi. Georgia had proclaimed independence after the fall of the USSR, and the Abkhazians demanded sovereignty too. Georgian troops were approaching the border. Already researchers from the Institute were making a break for Sochi. The sun was scorching the Caucasus. Nationalist songs resounded in the city. The Institute employees were neglecting the animals, and the cages became more and more foul. At night, Spiroberg and I made our way through halls that felt like they were closing in, and we spoke less and less, pacing through the building in silence. On August 12, 1992, when I heard gunfire in the distance, I took Spiroberg by the hand and I begged him to follow me. He shook his head, and I didn't insist. I knew he would stay with the apes.

In some corner of the Institute, I would see a crack snaking down a wall and chunks of plaster falling. Spiroberg and I only met rarely at McGill now, and always at the museum. I felt like we were surrounded by clumsily stuffed animals, by lynxes and hyenas that were emptying out, and whose glass eyes didn't fit their sockets. Every day I woke up with a crippling headache. The migraines lingered for hours, but I could never get back to sleep. One night there was a macaque staring at me from the foot of my bed. The animal had a belly wound, and its mouth was bleeding too. That night I couldn't find Spiroberg, not at McGill and not in Sukhumi, and the next day the war swept through the city. The bombs left it in ruins. Later we heard about rapes, murder, ethnic cleansing. Monkeys were shot; some were caught and leashed like pets by warlords.

When the Institute was attacked, I was there alone. I was looking for Spiroberg. I heard gunshots, the drubbing of bullets and shells against the walls. Dust filled the hallways as I ran. Outside, I got to the monkey pen and ran into a jumble of pelts, dozens of chimps and mandrills.

Their odour filled my nostrils, their screams filled my ears. When a bomb whistled, I threw myself down; the noise made my head explode. When I got up, the decapitated body of a chimpanzee lay next to me, prone in the dust. The bomb had ripped out the fence, and the apes were already gone. I hurried after them, into the forest. I ran but I couldn't catch up. Sometimes I thought I saw them crawling under the trees or climbing in the branches, but I was probably imagining things. Thinking back, I also think there was a giant black monkey crawling on all fours, its tail curling above the trees and its guts bleeding. I ran, I disappeared. I thought I was dying. At times I didn't know if I was a man or an ape. I stumbled over roots and tore my knees and hands, darting among branches that whipped at my face, crawling along a cuff of thorns. My heartbeat was pounding in my head as I left Montreal and Sukhumi behind, sinking into the forest as daylight faltered.

In the dim, dark night I moved blind, the cries of animals sounding all around me. I fell, a pathetic biped, tumbling to the bottom of a ravine. Both my legs were broken. I knew I would never get up again, that I would die alone, surrounded by the night beasts. I had no sense of who I was anymore, me or Spiroberg. At dawn, an old mandrill with a red and blue face and a thick mane watched over my last sleep in the forest where it had escaped from the Primate Institute, the forest where it would now live and then die.

I don't know if I ever really woke up, after that. I still live in my apartment in the Ghetto, with a vague sense that I exist. I never see Spiroberg in my sleep anymore. But a one-eyed baboon perched on my desk looks at me, and behind the window, hanging from the highest branches of a tree, swings a headless gibbon. Sometimes I share my bed with a gorilla whose body is rotting and some days when I come back from work or when I head out to study I have the impression that I'm living in a fragile reality on the verge of collapse. The world is too fast, and I cannot fathom the future. The newspapers and political news sites are full of stories about the thousands of refugees drowned in the Mediterranean, of others chased through forests across the Balkans and into Central Europe, of a hospital bombed in Homs, of an animal clone that died in agony. Of the surfeit of progress and disasters to come. I think back to the ruins of Sukhumi. The buildings on Milton or University seem to be collapsing too. In my throat I hold the taste of dust, in my nostrils the scent of animals, and it seems to me that Sukhumi has claimed all of reality for itself.

SHIPWRECKS

ON THE THIRD DAY OF THE CRUISE, Antoine remembered a short story he'd read two years earlier in a literary magazine. The author's name escaped him, if it had even registered at the time. The story was about a shipwreck.

A man wakes, stranded on the beach on a rocky island, and recounts his efforts to survive—how he laps rainwater from hollows in the stone, hunts crabs with stones and eats them raw. But it seems unlikely that he can survive for very long. It rains for the first few days, and then clears. There's not a cloud in the sky and the sun dries up the island, where no springs or streams flow. Only a few reptiles and birds live there. The crab meat makes the man sick. He's feverish, and the sun burns his skin.

One morning, in the distance, he spots a giant fish on the beach. Coming nearer, he sees that it's a shark, still alive, its tail flapping weakly on the sand. The gills sigh open near the mouth, and now and again the fish's jaw jerks and snaps shut over nothing.

The man flings heavy stones at the animal's head to finish it off. He's hungry, and slices open the shark's belly with the edge of a shell to cut out pieces of meat, eating them raw. His arms and clothes are stained with blood, he has blood on his face. Soon after, sitting on the sand, he's nauseated and vomits a whitish substance, which washes away in the waves. The man curses his lack of restraint, the voracity with which he gorged on the fish, his belly too weak to digest such a large amount of food. His mouth is pasty, he's thirsty, and the sun beats down on his skull as the shark's blood flakes off his skin.

The rest of the story seemed surreal. The castaway's fever gets worse. He's lost track of the sun, the difference between day and night. A chasm opens up beneath him. He thinks about the void, he thinks he's sinking. The disembowelled shark rots slowly on the beach. At times he thinks he hears the flick of its jaw inviting him out to sea. In the ocean, other worlds would open up, another possible life. The man comes to see the shark as a fleshy Trojan horse that can carry him off to places unknown, beyond the reach of mere mortals. He himself no longer seems human. His body is skeletal, his hair tangled with sand and blood, his face drawn and red. He looks like a feeble ancient deity as he drags the shark closer to the water's edge. Under a sky drenched in stars he pries open the fish's belly with both hands and slips in, pulling the wound closed behind him. And waits for the tide to come in, as if he were aboard a boat that might actually set sail.

Antoine didn't know what to make of the story. The shipwrecked man in the putrefied body of the shark sank into the ocean, into death. His madness gave him the illusion of escape. Or maybe it was a deliberate suicide, and he was inventing a tale for himself to forget the coming of death.

He'd long since stopped thinking about it, and was surprised that it came back to him now, on a ship on the Aegean Sea.

They'd been at sea going on three days and were approaching the island of Paros. It was the third time Antoine and Marie had taken a cruise to the Greek islands. They had also done the West Indies and the South Pacific. They had even gone to Antarctica, among the glaciers, but they preferred Greece: the scenery, the climate, the wines they sipped on shore while the ship was docked. The trip felt familiar; they weren't worried about the itinerary and thought only glancingly about their next stopovers.

It was the summer of 2015. Clouds were scarce and the sun beamed down on the *Gold of the Seas.* The passengers' sunscreen-slick skin glowed. This was their third trip to Greece, and Antoine and Marie had chosen a luxury vessel, more intimate than the huge cruise ships they'd travelled on before. The little touches were an immediate delight—the attentions of the crew, evenings in the jacuzzi under the stars, how easy it was to connect with other passengers. The ship, which was over a hundred metres long, felt both spacious and private.

Marie had been doing better since the beginning of the trip. She was still taking her medication, and Antoine wouldn't have dared suggest she stop, but she seemed to have put the depression behind her. She didn't even mention her father's recent death in a car accident.

Other than a few details, their trip to Paros was exactly like the previous year's visit. They ambled among the limewashed houses, admired the blue domes of the churches, the rocks carved out by the waves. As they had the year before, they ate calamari and drank white wine near the port of Naoussa. Antoine looked at Marie. She was beautiful, and he had the unexpected thought that he loved her.

That evening they shared a table with a young English couple on the deck of the *Gold of the Seas*. The air was warm and the sky was full of stars. The woman's name was Helen, and she owned an assisted reproductive technology laboratory. The man, Peter, ran an advertising agency.

The day's tour of the island had been hot and busy. Everyone wanted to drink, and tongues gradually loosened. It was the English couple's first cruise. The whole thing made them smile. The tourist brochure had boasted of adventure on the high seas but as far as they were concerned there was no longer such a thing as adventure. "The world is fully mapped," Peter said. "You can stroll the streets of Baghdad or Moscow on Google Maps, or zip from Berlin to Paris in just a few days, then pop over to Cancún or Johannesburg. Adventure is now the realm of advertising copy. I don't even know whether to complain about it. Back in the day, sea travel was terrible: the scurvy, the dying of thirst, the seething humanity."

Peter's pat assessment left no room for disagreement. But for Antoine, cruises were a way to travel without having to think. He could enjoy his early retirement. He read for hours and traded books with the other passengers. He liked watching the sea, its infinite expanse, the depths that could scarcely be guessed at, the animals that broke the surface now and again before disappearing. He also liked the cozy cabin, the closeness with Marie, their lovemaking, which sometimes, for an evening, was as intense as it had been in the early years. Above all, sailing was a childhood fulfillment. It reminded him of the pirate stories his father used to read him, and which he'd read and reread. The books had long gone out of print, and Antoine had even reissued some of the titles when he inherited his father's publishing business. The pirates were savage, the tales bursting with blood and sweat, bodies tossed into the sea. Antoine imagined them drifting among the waves and vanishing slowly below.

His own life had been a bit of a shipwreck at times. The publishing house had teetered on the brink of bankruptcy more than once. Marie ran her business as best she could despite the depression that plagued her. He didn't say it, but at times he felt like he was sinking. His sleep was increasingly fragile. Often when he opened his eyes at dawn he couldn't go back to sleep. He began remembering his dreams, which he had always so quickly forgotten. Scraps of dreams, torn and faded, stayed with him. He kept bits and pieces, persistent images that haunted him: the recurring corpse of his father, who'd died many years before Marie's, and about whom he almost never spoke; being lost in a huge publishing house, its walls buckling under the weight of books.

On the first night of the cruise, he dreamed that he was walking through that publishing house, carrying a stack of books he was trying to shelve. Water poured down the walls. It soaked his feet and welled around his ankles. The place was flooding steadily. Later he was swimming in a room wallpapered with maps. The space between the water and the ceiling was getting narrower. He was afraid to drown, to suffocate to death. Under the water, Marie clung to his feet.

Antoine never told anybody his dreams. They were so much psychic mud flowing out of his mind, yet they reminded him of the stories he loved. They touched him in a similar way, stirring up feelings he'd never known.

On the fifth night of the cruise, after a boozy evening spent with Helen and Peter, he went to bed drunk. The ceiling above him was spinning and he closed his eyes but couldn't sleep. He grabbed some sleeping pills from Marie's purse, but threw them up almost immediately. Later, still unable to sleep, he went up to the deck. It was a beautiful night. The deck was empty. Antoine leaned against the guardrail. The starry sky's reflection in the sea was warped by the swell. Antoine thought he might be sick again, but nothing came up. That night the sea was an abyss, the sky drowning in it, and there was no way to be sure the ship was still sailing, its hull grazed by the waves. *The sea no longer exists*, he thought to himself, while the emptiness growing inside him seemed to overwhelm what was real.

The feeling of emptiness faded with the light. Antoine went back to his room and laid down next to Marie. She hadn't noticed he'd been gone. When she got up, his eyes were still open. He told her he wouldn't be going up for breakfast, and heard her leave. At last, he managed to get some sleep.

They spent the whole day at sea, off the Turkish coast. The sky was clear. The passengers had gathered, mostly in couples, along the guardrail. They were looking at the waves, looking for something, the head of a monk seal peeping out, or a pod of dolphins. When Antoine found Marie on deck, the news had spread to a hum: there had been a shipwreck. An Australian passenger had found out on his phone, by satellite, that a boat overloaded with Libyan refugees had foundered just a few miles away. Hundreds of victims. *How awful*, the passengers whispered. Many wandered back to their cabins. Others watched the water, picturing human bodies floating in the distance. The captain offered everyone a drink. The speakers crackled out some Charles Aznavour, then Marvin Gaye. The laughter sounded forced. People spoke in muted voices. By late afternoon, it was obvious most people were drunk, and even more so at nightfall. Antoine, Marie, Helen and Peter were seated at the same table again. Crab was served. After the meal, a few couples ventured out onto the dance floor, but with less conviction than usual. The dinner crowd thinned out, though the passengers who remained seemed determined to see out the night. People were switching tables, sharing bottles. An old man staggering around fell and was just barely caught. Marie went to bed earlier than usual, and Antoine stayed alone with Helen and Peter. They ordered more champagne. Peter's mouth was pasty. He ranted about porous borders and those who cross them through hill and dale, their bodies torn apart by brambles and barbed wire. About other borders, lines drawn in the sea, and all those who come across with their futile aspirations. Antoine thought back to the adventure novels of his childhood and imagined himself sailing above the waves and sinking below.

When he got back to the cabin, Marie was crying. He was completely inebriated and collapsed next to her without being able to console her. He felt himself going under. There were wrecks everywhere and Antoine's arms flailed, pale and pitiful in the impossible darkness, as he lost the ability to hope.

JELLYFISH

A THICK LAYER OF SNOW covered the grass around his house in Trois-Rivières the day the insect lodged in Michel's throat. He was in Mexico at the time, on a beach in the Yucatán. The haze of a dream lingered in his head. All he could remember was a thick fog, and his mother's body, gaunt and oversized. She'd been dead for a long time. The night was hot and humid. Earlier he had woken up in his hotel room, next to Sarah, who was breathing softly, perspiration beading on her skin. Michel's sheets were damp with sweat. He got up and went outside. His feet sank into the sand as he walked toward the waves. He sat on the shore, looking at the foam breaking less than a metre away, and soon the ocean wet his feet and legs. A little farther along, he saw lights shining in the sea, blurry shapes distorted by the swirling waves. He laughed without knowing what he found so funny, and he didn't feel the insect that landed on his tongue right then and crawled inside his mouth. Around him, glistening jellyfish dragged out onto the sand.

Two days later, they came back to Quebec. The January cold was staggering: the roads were slick, and an icy wind blew drifts across the highway. Cars had skidded off the road and sat braced in the ditch. Michel was driving along the 40 to Trois-Rivières, tanned but bundled up, because the heat in his Acura didn't work very well. In the passenger seat, Sarah grumbled and flipped through radio stations. As soon as they got home, Michel spiked a fever. He took a couple of pills, and went to bed. As he slept he felt antennae burrow into his cerebral cortex and stay there. The insect's legs grew inside him like roots, sliding into his nervous system and his bloodstream until they reached his feet and hands. When he woke, he still had a fever. His tongue was heavy. His mouth was dry, even after he had something to drink. He didn't go to work on the first day after his holiday. When he was home alone he barely got out of bed, but when he did he looked at himself in the mirror and found his skin oily and ugly. His baldness stretched over his skull. He had deep, dark circles under his eyes. The scars of long-ago acne still marked his face, even in his forties. When he splashed water on his face, it seemed to run down his shiny skin without cleaning it. He went back to bed, lay back down under the damp blankets. When he closed his eyes, he could see the jellyfish glistening in the night. He thought they were crashing around him, and he remembered the fireflies he used to catch when he went partying as a teenager in a sand quarry near Trois-Rivières. The fireflies' crushed abdomens left a twinkling powder between his fingers, and he watched the lights die out while he drank beer.

He didn't go back to work the next day either. Sarah was worried, but he refused to go to the doctor. It was nothing, he said. Just the flu, a holiday hangover. He was tired. He needed some sleep. As he slept, on that second day of his extended vacation, he felt that his tongue distended, slipped between his lips, slid down to his stomach and then to the foot of his bed, where it coiled in the dust. Bedbugs, ants, and silverfish came and went between the tip of his tongue and the floor. Michel did not return to work that week.

He finally agreed to see a doctor, if only to justify his prolonged absence from work, and the doctor confirmed the fever. Michel needed to rest, and to take ibuprofen regularly. Michel spent his days sleeping. He seldom got out of bed. He had no appetite, and little interest in life other than sleeping. During his waking hours, he sometimes read books and comic books. He rummaged through a cupboard that he hadn't opened for years and found a box with comics from when he was a teenager. He read a few pages of *The Incredible Hulk* and *Spider-Man*. Wilson Fisk crushed a skull between his palms and Doctor Strange turned a bank robber into an alien reptile. Each time, after reading a bit, he went back to sleep, exhausted. He read not only American comic books, but also fanzines from when he was older, during his college years. He looked at the characters. Their bodies were shapeless, and their heads were huge. Occasionally they wielded disproportionate penises. In one story, a father cut up his twin sons with an axe and burned them at the stake, and Michel thought of childhood fairy tales, the shadows of animals lurking in the woods, in alleyways, or hidden under his bed or behind the radiator. Michel let his eyelids drop. Almost imperceptibly he felt another being inhabiting his body, the legs planted in his flesh, wings flapping softly under his rib cage. The insect he had swallowed in Mexico had grown to tremendous proportions, developing inside him as if Michel were pregnant. Michel wasn't always aware of its presence, he mostly tried to ignore it, but when he slept he could feel it, clear and distinct. He would open his mouth and stick out his tongue, as if for a doctor asking him to say *ahhh*. The insect's leg would appear sticking out between his lips, or else its proboscis, or the tip of a wing covered in scales. Never the antennae, which remained plunged in Michel's cortex. He wouldn't go back to work, he thought to himself, but he wouldn't live like the humans either. He wanted something exotic, travel, the beach, tropical countries, and above all faraway lands. Faint impulses made him want to push beyond what was real. These were plans he made only for himself and the insect. For the first time, perhaps, he no longer felt a fear of death, that muffled but sovereign fear he had denied for a long time, although it had always been there. Nor did he feel any ambition, any desire to make something of himself.

He only wanted to disappear, to withdraw from the human race. The insect spread out under his skin and he sometimes thought that there were others too, scurrying on the outside, a surge of tiny arthropods swarming from his toes to his head, scampering across his limbs, slipping between his fingers, circling around his belly. The offspring, he thought, were the fruits of his congress with the insect, a relationship he was experiencing from within, exploring its long-term potential.

Michel never did go back to work. His fever never abated. He left one day with the insect, abandoning his job and his wife. He had surrendered, Sarah often said. She seemed to understand. And some nights, while she slept, she thought she could feel an octopus or an eel growing inside her. She stretched out her arms. Her fingers writhed like the nubs of tentacles. Her eyes fluttered like the glint of amoebas in the depths. When she woke, alone in her house in Trois-Rivières, she found herself craving the beaches of Mexico once again. The winter dragged on, and snow covered the garden and seemed to bury the whole world as it waited for spring—for a new awakening, for beetles, butterflies, and bumblebees to seethe out of the earth, fly away, to rustle near human ears. Yet it sometimes felt like the winter was expanding into spring and summer.

The sky is icy, Sarah thought one morning in May. The ground is frozen. The insects haven't woken up. And she remembered that night in Mexico when Michel had gotten up in the middle of the night. She imagined that she had gotten up after him, looking out the hotel window at the sea. She could see the flicker of lights cresting on the beach and fading. Sarah hesitated. Suddenly she wanted to die. Her sheets were cold, her body was tense. She could hear the crash of the waves as all around her the iridescent jellyfish slowly went dark.

THE DOG WITHOUT A HEAD

CLARA'S DOG was born without a head one July morning, during the hottest days of summer. The mother had whelped by the cedar hedge in one of the few shady spots in the yard, flies buzzing around her. The bitch died as her only baby was being born. Paul, the fat guy who lived nearby, had come to watch. Maybe, Paul suggested, the animal's head had stayed trapped in the mother's body, in her womb. Paul's twin sons laughed when they heard his explanation. When they got back home, they drew pictures in marker of huge bellies filled with animal heads. But Clara held the puppy in her hands, talking to him where his head would have been, as if she'd been whispering into the shell of an ear. The little dog fell asleep in Clara's arms as the girl's parents buried the mother under the cedars, marking the grave with a subtle white cross.

Clara's new companion was lively and playful. The dog was deaf and blind, but quite in tune with the outside world, as if he had a sixth sense—maybe the ability some say allows dogs to see ghosts or to guess at the feelings of humans, our fear or suffering. And so Clara's pet stood alongside her on the threshold of adolescence. She was eleven years old, all inner turmoil, dreams, and worries. As soon as the dog woke up, he would run to greet her, and she held him against her and felt his heartbeat.

Clara's parents were happy that their daughter had a friend. They led busy lives; both worked long hours and lots of overtime. On weekends they redecorated the house together, puttering at it endlessly, and every Saturday they had friends over for dinner, eating and drinking for hours. They had little time for their child, who appreciated the dog's company.

Clara spent her days in the garden with the dog, confiding in him as if he understood her. Sometimes she placed her ear against the animal's belly, listening to the swarming rumble inside. She imagined a head in there, and she wondered what the dog was thinking. Or she would lie down in the grass, putting her human head where his would have been. When the puppy lay on his mother's grave, she believed with him that they could feel her presence, reaching along with the little dog for the memory of maternal warmth—a glow of well-being, and the vague sensation of dying with her as he was born.

When fall came, she didn't like leaving him alone at home. But he was so excited to see her when she got home from school, deliriously happy, rolling in the grass around her as the twins, who were dropped off by the school bus at the same time as she was, looked on. They would walk by, snickering, and every evening, through a gap in the cedars, they spied on the girl and her dog: this child left to her own devices, who seemed cast aside by her parents, and her strange headless animal, the dog she talked to all the time, that way she had of putting her head on the dog's belly, the afternoons they spent by the grave, such a blaring reminder of death, in an empty grassy patch without a swimming pool or a basketball court. The older of the twins liked to think about what the dog's head would have looked like, whether he'd had one, if it had decomposed in the mother's body. Once he suddenly chuckled out loud when he decided that it might have been a human head.

They forgot whose idea it was first, but one Monday in September the two brothers blew up a balloon, glued strips of paper mâché, and painted them, shaping a head more or less reminiscent of a dog's, though it could also have belonged to some other animal. The features were grotesque: the left eye was disproportionately large, the right ear drooped like a tongue. They lobbed their handiwork over the hedge. Every day of the week, they threw more of them, like balls, canine heads at first, then the heads of other critters—bears, cats, hyenas—and of odd, unidentifiable creatures. There was even a human head. Every day, the paper mâché heads tumbled in the grass not far from the bitch's grave while the twins cried, *Here's a head for your dog! A head for your dog!* And every day, Clara stomped on yet another head with both feet, and shoved it with the rest into a garbage bag, to drop by the curb the following Monday, on an unnervingly sunny day much like the day the dog was born.

He died one Friday that fall when he was hit by the school bus bringing Clara home from school. As he did every day, the dog had run out to meet her. The sky was bright. The children were restless on the hot September afternoon, shouting and laughing, and distracting the driver, who yelled at them to shut up. No one saw the dog get hit by the bus, no one heard the thump or saw him hurled onto the sidewalk in front of Clara's house. She and the twins found him as they came out. Red pooled where his head might have been. There were flies landing already. The children formed a circle around the puddle. Their brains seemed heavy. The sun was bursting in the twins' skulls, and it shone hot on their little neighbour's head. Everyone felt the weight of the blood. It covered Clara's fingers as she picked up the dog. It smeared on her sleeves and stained her shoes. Later she wiped it on her shirt. While she dug, the twins stayed on their side of the cedars, watching her in silence; they were still standing there when their neighbour's parents planted another small white cross. That evening, as Clara cried, Paul's sons cried too, in secret.

The days after were hot. Summer was taking its time. Skinned knees bled in the schoolyard, and the bus smelled like children's sweat. Every time they got off the bus, Clara and her neighbours relived the red asphalt and the dead dog, and they walked away quietly to their respective sides of the hedge.

One evening, the twins crossed the hedge. With Clara, they knelt at the dog's grave. They had brought a head. It was beautiful, the ears were dropped low, the tongue sticking out. It looked as if it might bark. The next day, placed in the grass, the head gleamed beneath the wide, burning sky.

FROM MY TUMOUR WITH LOVE

SOMETIMES WHEN I'M DRUNK I send too many lovelorn emails, which I reread the next day, humiliated. One evening I phoned, too, though I had no idea where on the planet I might be calling. No answer, as usual. Last month, Luce, a mutual friend, had a chance encounter in Borneo, where they were both on holiday. They were walking on the beach when they ran into each other. The sun was dazzling, apparently, and my tumour was breathtakingly beautiful.

My tumour doesn't answer my calls or my emails, but sometimes it does take the time to write me a letter. I've gotten letters postmarked in Mali, Peru, Kazakhstan, Slovakia. Sometimes I fan them all out on my kitchen table, I move them around, I read them, I reread them out of order. It chokes me up every time, though I'm not sure if it's from nostalgia or actual sorrow. The letters make me both happy and sad. Reading them is reading the story of my life.

*

Dear T*,

Yesterday I went on an expedition along the Amazon River. The heat was stifling, and the mosquitoes multitudinous. I could hear howler monkeys screaming in the distance. My head felt heavy, like it was full of water, as if my brain were a sponge that had to be wrung out and the rest of my body was dry; my skin like parchment. I slathered on citronella and moisturizer. I drank lots of water and felt that the river was also flowing inside me. The captain had organized a party that evening. There are about ten of us passengers. They'd draped the boat with lanterns. Almost right away, a stranger offered me a cocktail, which I drank in one gulp. He bought me another. He's a rich Azerbaijani heir, a shareholder in an oil company. A good-looking man. He speaks with a bewitching accent. Like me, he's travelling around the world, but his route is all planned out in advance, and the end of his journey too. I did not let myself be seduced. I told him I wouldn't go with him to Bolivia. Later I heard him snoring in his sleep. His cabin is next to mine. The heat was unbearable. His body must have been coated with sweat, his sheets soaked beneath the mosquito netting. I would have liked to run my hand over his chest, to hold him, feel my sweat mix with his, but I stayed in my cabin. I thought of his heart beating in the night, locked up in his rib cage, beating since the start of his life as if it had to beat for the rest of time.

Today I went into the jungle with a group of American and British tourists. Outlandishly shaped mushrooms grew among the roots, tipping their caps to sprinkle their spores. Our guide told me that one year a Canadian got lost during the outing. He had ventured alone into the jungle and disappeared. Miraculously, he was found the next day. His skin was covered with stings, and his face was red and swollen. He couldn't open his eyes. I wish I could have seen him. I would've liked to sketch him. Did you know I'd started drawing again? Sometimes I remember the portraits I used to make of you, your body and mine attached to each other, back when we were always together. Maybe you've kept some of them. I don't know *what I did with mine. To tell the truth, I don't hold on to things anymore, I haven't for a long time.*

I'm going to leave Brazil the first chance I get. Apparently in Africa there are cities so big that they brim over into the sea. And I want to see the Pacific Islands. I remember that beach where the two of us walked together, our shadows drawn out on the sand as the cormorants seemed to drown in the waves in the distance.

I think about you often. Last night I saw you again in a dream: you were beautiful, your body so big, your tongue fluttered sublime things that I forgot when I woke up.

They say it's better not to live with regrets. Sometimes I let myself go a bit.

Affectionately,

Your tumour

For the first few months it was only a redness, purplish, then a bit of swelling, then a stump-like growth, a sort of rough outline of an arm on my shoulder. My tumour liked to say that we met by accident, but I think it chose to take shape on my skin. I say a stump, but it could have been a head, to the left of mine, as if I were bicephalous.

Shortly after my tumour appeared, I stopped working. I'd saved a lot of money—I'd been working for over twenty years straight, no wife or children, and I spent almost nothing. We went on vacation together. The beach in Samoa stretched out as far as the eye could see. The waves could be huge; I can still hear the din as they crashed. Crabs shuffled around us, and their shells brushed against my feet. When my tumour and I dove in, the salt water stung its purple head, and it glistened next to me in the sun.

Its evolution was inconsistent, unpredictable. I liked watching it grow. It would stay the same size for weeks, then double in a single night. Every morning I turned my head and looked at my shoulder: the round shape, the veins protruding, and the colours, every shade of red, changing from week to week, wine red to ochre to purple. Each new shape was more beautiful than the last. I told my tumour this, and it was grateful.

Sometimes I could hear it whispering in my head. It was describing the perpetual rotation of Earth, the cycle of the seasons, the infinite darkness of the depths and of the sky. It told me about its body and mine, the blood flowing in my arteries, my lungs filling with air. One day it would all stop. But it seemed to me that it was also in my blood, and I thought it would gradually invade my whole body, settling in my arms and my legs, in my belly and then in my head, in each of my cells and neurons, until we were one.

In Samoa, we lay in the sand together, in the sun or under the stars. I drew lines in the sand with my fingertips or with a stick. I traced my tumour's outline or mine, then others, figures whose appearance, each time, seemed to be a distorted reflection of mine. These drawings were inspired by my tumour. It sprouted on my shoulder, but it also got into my head. It was a genius, it could see life's big truths. Every day with my tumour, things seemed more accurate and more authentic. I was no longer afraid of what the future would bring.

Yet little by little the fear caught up. After a week on the island, a violent storm forced us to hide out in our hotel room and muddied the sea. One morning I woke up with a fever, which wouldn't break for the next few days even when the weather turned nice again. My tumour wasn't as chatty as before. The lump on my shoulder got harder and became painful. I lost my appetite, I was impossibly thirsty.

My mouth was all pasty, and I had a hard time waking up.

On the tenth night of fever, I hallucinated that I was the tumour, a tumour with a bulging head like a misshapen mushroom eaten away by worms. I thought my head was gone, replaced by my tumour's.

The next day, the sun seemed colossal to me, disproportionate. I had a crushing migraine. I didn't leave my hotel room all day, but I couldn't fall asleep until around midnight.

When I woke, the sky was crammed with stars. I was nauseated, and my shoulder burned. I went for a walk on the beach, the foam soaking my feet. I remember the birds were screaming. I threw up, and my tumour comforted me. My vomit washed into the waves. The pain in my shoulder was sharp, and I worried that it would spread, that I would lose the strength to live. I thought of the scalpel, of going under the knife. I wanted to get rid of the bump I'd been talking to, that second head. I walked through the night, I threw up again. I knew I'd be heading home as soon as possible—which is to say, already I was leaving my tumour behind, and giving up an essential part of my existence. I remembered the happiness when we met, the incredible times we'd shared, the feeling of love, the illusion of a life that would last forever.

When I got back, it was deep winter and freezing cold. Not a single snowflake fell. My house in Blainville seemed too big and too empty. I had stopped speaking to my tumour, nor did I hear its voice resonate in my skull, but as I called the doctor, I remembered that it was beautiful, I thought that I was in love, that maybe I'd never been in love before, that I wouldn't ever love again.

After the operation, it was just a few weeks before I got the first letter. My tumour had mailed it from Samoa, taunting me. The second arrived from the Maldives. Letters were sent from South America—Brazil, Argentina, Uruguay. I don't know how it ended up in Africa, whether it travelled by plane or by boat, but after that, my tumour's correspondence reached me from Mozambique, and then from Tanzania. My tumour had gone bipedal. From the letters, I imagined its elegance, seductive but as deadly as ever. Without my tumour, I didn't feel like I was living anymore. To tell the truth, I felt like I was dying. I looked at my face in the bathroom mirror. I imagined eternal life: growing old forevermore, my nose and ears expanding imperceptibly over centuries, becoming gigantic, like the trunks and ears of elephants, and dragging in the dust, in a distant future into which humanity would perpetuate itself, immortal—a tumour with feet and hands.

I was thinking about the one who got away, who left me because I wanted it to go. Since my tumour had gone, I'd been alone in my house in the midst of this long winter. The rare time I went out, I talked about my tumour to my friends and family, others who might have known it. Together we looked for it online, for personal comments, some mention. We found my tumour's email and phone number. On Google Maps we tried, and failed, to retrace its steps.

Recently, in one of its letters, my tumour described the steppes at the border of Georgia and Azerbaijan—kilometres without a single human, a paucity of trees, the pleated earth. In another, it told me about a party in an abandoned building in Istanbul. It had painted my face on the wall, it said, a portrait twice its size, which it had been able to do by climbing on the shoulders of a young Russian it had met in a restaurant in the Bosporus. My tumour described the colours to me—the sparkling red, the immaculate blue which it then daubed over with black—and the gargantuan head, with a red and green brain that looked almost extraterrestrial. In another letter, it told me about its dreams: its naked body next to mine and my arms stretched out, my belly too and my head, my huge body prostrate, surrounded by trash.

For several weeks I didn't get any letters, and then one suddenly arrived, postmarked in Tbilisi. Others, a few days apart, came from the Balkans: Bosnia, Croatia, Albania, the Greek islands. Nothing again for almost three weeks before a letter came from Saint Pierre and Miquelon, and another from Rimouski. My tumour was near. I wanted it. Standing in front of the mirror I looked for its presence; sitting at my kitchen table I read its words:

Do you remember, the night we met, you were alone, lying in your bed, asleep. You dreamed you were lying in the middle of a ruined city. Crows landed on your skin like mosquitoes. Your body had putrefied in your sleep and the crows gradually ate you up, piercing their beaks into your elastic skin. That was the first time I drew you. I'm still drawing you today. I see you on the beach where the jellyfish have washed up. This is not your portrait as you are today; it is a portrait of days to come, and it is a truer likeness than your own life.

I would've liked to answer, but there was nothing to say except that I loved my tumour, and everything it said was true.

It wrote to me again from Baltimore, Panama, Macau, and I cried as I read the letters, hoping for its return.

*

Today, when my doctor said the word *metastasis,* I smiled. Then I got worried, I didn't know if it was my tumour again in a new form, or another, a stranger. The doctor talked about chemotherapy. I flew to Berlin, then Madrid, then Singapore. I brought all the letters in my suitcase. My tumour had told me about the blistering sun in Sinai, children starving to death in the war, snow so cold and fine you would have thought it could penetrate your skin, species that are going extinct and will never reappear. In its last letter, my tumour wrote:

On the beach, in Rapa Iti, I saw a gigantic octopus washed up on the tide. I lay down next to it. I thought of you and how unreliable reality is. I didn't know what to make of life, and I told myself that I would rather have died than be a tumour for all eternity, reborn from one disease to the next. I recalled the days we spent together. Those were the best days of my life.

QC FICTION

Current & Upcoming Books

Visit **qcfiction.com** for details and to subscribe
to a full season of QC Fiction titles.

Printed by Imprimerie Gauvin
Gatineau, Québec